# The
# Rescued
# Kitten

# Other titles by Holly Webb

## *The Hounds of Penhallow Hall:*

## *Winter Stories:*

## *Animal Stories:*

# The Rescued Kitten

Holly Webb
Illustrated by Sophy Williams

For the real Edie and Barbie. Thank you so much for telling me your wonderful story.

www.hollywebbanimalstories.com

STRIPES PUBLISHING
An imprint of the Little Tiger Group
1 Coda Studios, 189 Munster Road,
London SW6 6AW

A paperback original
First published in Great Britain in 2018

Text copyright © Holly Webb, 2018
Illustrations copyright © Sophy Williams, 2018
Author photograph copyright © Nigel Bird

ISBN: 978-1-84715-918-2

The right of Holly Webb and Sophy Williams to be
identified as the author and illustrator of this work
respectively has been asserted by them in accordance
with the Copyright, Designs and Patents Act, 1988.

A CIP catalogue record for this book is available
from the British Library.

Printed and bound in the UK.

10 9 8 7 6 5 4 3 2 1

# Chapter One

"This week seems to have gone on for ages. I'm so glad it's the weekend." Edie rolled her shoulders under the straps of her school bag and gave a huge sigh.

Layla nodded. "I know. Sometimes I think Mr Bennett makes Fridays hard on purpose. He knows we all just want to get home. We did too much writing today, way too much." She shuddered.

Edie giggled. "And too much thinking. Are you doing anything this weekend? Want to come over to mine tomorrow?"

Layla nodded. "Sounds great. I've got swimming tonight but nothing else."

The two girls lived almost next door to each other, in a group of houses that had once been old farm buildings. Each house had its own little garden at the back, but there was a shared courtyard in the middle of the houses, which meant there was usually a group of children around.

Up until this year, one of their mums or dads had always walked them to school, but luckily for Edie and Layla, a footpath led from their houses along the edge of some fields to the main village, where their school was. Now they were in Year Five, they were allowed to walk there and back by themselves.

The girls weren't far from home, following the footpath past a wheat field. They were keeping to the side, in the shelter of the hedge, out of the spitting rain. It was close to the end of the summer term but it had been a damp sort of day, not very summery at all.

"Is that a bird?" Edie asked, stopping suddenly.

"Where?" Layla stopped, too, peering up the track. They quite often saw pheasants stalking across the path, or rabbits. But she couldn't see anything now.

"I'm sure I can hear a noise." Edie turned round slowly, trying to work out where it was coming from. Maybe it was a bird that had fallen out of its nest. It was a bit late in the year for nesting birds, but she knew some birds laid more eggs after their first chicks had flown. So it could be a fledgling stuck on the ground. "A squeaking sound. Can't you hear it?" She crouched down. The noise seemed to be coming from somewhere to the side of the path.

"Oh… Yeah, I think so…" Layla crouched, too, frowning a little.

"I think it was coming from the hedge. But it's stopped now…" Edie could feel her heart starting to thump harder. When she'd first heard the noise, it had just been something she'd wanted to investigate, but now she was worried. The squeaking had sounded thin and weak and now it had stopped, as though whoever was making it had given up – like they didn't even have the strength to ask for help any more.

"I'm pretty sure it was over here," Edie murmured, leaning in and parting the long damp grass. There was a hedge of straggly hawthorn bushes growing beyond the grass and wild flowers.

"Mind the wire," Layla said, looking over Edie's shoulder. "There's barbed wire under those bushes, I can see it. Don't get scratched."

Edie nodded. "I'll be careful. Oh! Did you hear that?"

Another tiny, breath-like squeak rang out. There definitely was something in the hedge, something that sounded little and lost.

"What is it?" Layla asked, in a worried voice.

Edie carefully pulled back the prickly branches and the two girls peered in.

"Oh no…" Layla whispered.

Under the branches of the hedge, dangling from the strands of barbed wire, was a limp little bundle of ginger fur.

The kitten could hear something coming. She didn't know that she was hearing children's voices – she didn't know what people were, she had never met any. She only knew her mother, her brother and her sisters, and that

they had left her here. She didn't
understand what was happening now.
Could it be her mother coming back
to find her? It didn't sound like her
mother. She moved softly, quickly, not
like this – not with noise and heavy
footsteps. The kitten wriggled a little,
unsure whether she should try again
to free herself before this strange thing
came any closer. But she couldn't
move. She was trapped and every time
she tried to pull herself away from the
thing that was holding her, she felt
weaker and weaker.

She needed help.

But if it wasn't her mother, what was
it? The kittens had heard foxes and
other animals sniffing around outside
the hollow tree where their mother

had made her little den, but they didn't know what the creatures were. They were so little that their mother was the only thing they really knew – the warmth of her curling up around them, her milk and the gentle way she licked them clean.

It must be her mother coming back to find her, the kitten decided. Her mother wouldn't abandon her like this. The kitten tried again to wriggle, and then mewed, as loud as she could. *Find me, help me, take me home, I'm frightened!*

Even though it was her loudest mew, the sound was still very faint. Hardly more than a squeak. She tried again, squeaking and tugging back against the wire as hard as she could. It bounced a little and she squeaked once more, with pain this time as the long fur on the back of her neck pulled and the wire pressed into her skin.

The noise was coming closer and she twisted her body, pulling to try and see what was making it, still calling faintly to her mother. But instead of a cat hurrying to rescue her, the kitten saw two frightened, wide-eyed faces. She wrenched at the wire again and the

cut on her neck went deeper. It hurt and she sagged down miserably. She was terrified and so, so tired.

She didn't understand. All she could do was close her eyes and hope that whatever this was would go away and then her mother would come.

# Chapter Two

"A kitten!" Edie breathed. "I thought it had to be a bird…"

Layla nodded. "Is it stuck?"

"Yeah, poor little thing." Edie wriggled a bit closer into the hedge, ignoring the thorny branches catching on her jacket and tangling in her hair. "I think it's her long fur – she's got it all tangled up in the barbed wire.

Oh, poor baby, she's actually cut her neck on it, too."

"Can you get her out?" Layla asked. "Do you want me to lift up the wire or something?"

Edie sat back on her heels for a moment. "I'm just thinking. Maybe we should go and fetch my mum? She'll know how to rescue the kitten without hurting her." She looked worriedly at the tiny kitten, wondering what to do. What she wanted was to get her off the wire as quickly as possible.

She seemed so small and fragile, stuck there, and the cut on her neck looked horrible. Edie's mum and dad were both vets, so it wasn't as if Edie hadn't seen sick animals before. Quite often if no one was able to look after a sick cat or dog at the surgery, Mum or Dad would bring them home, and Edie loved the chance to fuss over them and pretend she had a pet of her own. But she'd never seen a creature look so feeble and so clearly in pain.

As Edie looked at her, the kitten opened her eyes – tiny round green eyes – and stared back. She mewed, or at least she tried to but no sound came out. She didn't even have the strength left to mew, Edie realized.

"No, we need to get her out of there

right now," she muttered. "She's so weak. We need to get her back home so Mum can have a look at her." She reached tentatively towards the kitten, wondering if the little thing would scratch or bite – not to be nasty, just because she was so scared. But when Edie touched the clump of fur that was twisted up in the teeth of the wire, the kitten didn't try to fight. She just shuddered a little and opened her mouth in another heart-breaking silent mew.

Edie tried to pull at the clump of fur, but it was stuck so tightly that it didn't budge and she could feel the kitten flinching. "It's no good, I'm only hurting her," she whispered, looking round at Layla anxiously. "What are we going to do?"

"Scissors! I've got scissors in my pencil case!" Layla shrugged off her backpack and fished inside for her pencil case. "Here, look, and they're nice and sharp. You can just cut the fur away." She passed a pair of scissors to Edie and Edie leaned in closer to the kitten.

The tiny creature opened her eyes again, but when she saw Edie looming towards her, and the shiny blades of the scissors, she started to struggle.

"It's OK," Edie whispered. "We're trying to get you out of there."

"Is it working?" Layla asked worriedly, peering over Edie's shoulder.

"Yes ... nearly there." Edie snipped at the ginger fur. She cupped her left hand underneath the kitten to catch her and cut through the last chunk of fur. The kitten slumped into her hand, limp and floppy like a beanbag toy.

Edie passed the scissors to Layla and crept backwards, the kitten cupped in her hands. The tiny thing stirred and wriggled a little as she was brought out of the shadow of the hedge and into the light. The two girls stared down at her.

"She's so little," Layla whispered. "What's she doing here on her own?"

"I don't know." Edie cuddled the kitten against her school dress for a minute, trying to reach round to her backpack. "Ugh, I can't do this with one hand – can you get my cardigan out? We can wrap her up in it – I know it's not all that cold but you're supposed to keep tiny kittens warm and it was chilly under that hedge."

Layla found the cardigan and Edie wrapped the kitten up in it, so that just her little ginger face was peeping out. Her eyes were closed again and Edie was sure that wasn't a good sign. "She's got a cut on her front paw, too, did you see? Maybe she was trying to claw her way out of the wire. Come on – we'd better not run and bounce her around but we can walk fast."

Layla nodded and they hurried along the path with the kitten in Edie's arms.

"Mum! Mum!" Edie rang the doorbell for a second time and called in through the open front window.

"I was in the kitchen…" Edie's mum pulled open the door, rolling her eyes at the two girls. "I didn't take that long!"

"No, I know, sorry – Mum, look!" Edie held out the sad little bundle in her arms.

"Oh my goodness. Where did you find a kitten?" Edie's mum took the cardigan and looked down worriedly. "Was it hit by a car?" Then she looked up, confused. "No, you'd have gone to Dad at the surgery if you were by the road. So what happened?"

"We found her in a hedge. She was caught on some barbed wire. I had to cut her fur with Layla's scissors. Is she going to be OK?"

Edie's mum gently put the bundle on the kitchen table. The kitten was lying there, curled up on Edie's cardigan, not moving at all. Edie could just about see she was breathing but that was it.

"I don't know," her mum said slowly. "She could have been there for a while, you see, and she's very tiny. Maybe about five weeks old? That's very small to be away from her mother. Edie, can you get me a cardboard box out of the garage? Not a massive one – just something we can make into a nice little nest for the kitten."

When Edie came back with the box she saw that her mum had found a hot-water bottle and was filling it up. "We need to get her nice and warm," she explained. "Not too warm, though, we'll wrap the bottle in a towel. Edie, could you—" but Edie was already racing up the stairs to the airing cupboard. Her mum padded out the box with the hot-water bottle and the towel, and gently lifted the kitten inside. "I'm pretty sure we've still got some of that kitten milk from the last time we had kittens here," she murmured. Then she looked up at the girls. "Look, we'll do the best we can, of course we will, but you have to understand, she's very little and she's injured and shocked. She might not have the strength to get through this."

Edie swallowed and nodded, and she felt Layla's hand slip into hers. "We can try, though?" she whispered.

Her mum nodded. "Definitely. Just … don't get your hopes up too much."

The kitten blinked wearily. She was warm and she wasn't being jogged about any more. She wasn't caught up in the wire now either, she was somewhere soft and comfortable. That was good. The kitten flexed her tiny claws in and out of the towel, and a shiver ran over her. But her mother still hadn't come to find her and she was so hungry. And the wound on her neck hurt, and so did her paw. She was sure she wouldn't be able to walk on it, even if she had the energy to try.

What was happening? Where was her mother and why hadn't she come back?

# Chapter Three

Layla had to go home to get ready for her swimming lesson but she made Edie promise to call her later. "I still can't believe we found her," she murmured, as she backed reluctantly out of Edie's kitchen. "You will tell me what happens, won't you? I'll be home by six."

"I promise," Edie agreed. "We'd never have got her untangled from the wire without your scissors. She's your rescued kitten, too." She waved to Layla and hurried back into the kitchen. The kitten was snuggled into the towel that Edie's mum had put on the floor of the box, covering the hot-water bottle. Edie's mum had dressed her cut leg, and the bandage looked huge on her tiny paw.

"I've got that bear you can heat up in the microwave like a hot-water bottle," Edie suggested. "Shall I get it? The bottle isn't covering the whole box. There's a cold bit on one side."

Edie's mum shook her head. "No, that's good. She's too little for her body to warm up or cool down by itself, so the box needs a warm side and a cooler one. Once she's feeling warmer she'll move herself away from the hot-water bottle.

Hopefully, anyway." She was watching the kitten, frowning a little as the tiny creature lay slumped on the towel.

"Can't we give her some milk?" Edie asked. "Wouldn't that make her feel better?"

Her mum nodded. "It would. I just want to wait a little bit – she's so floppy, I think she's still cold. If she's been under that hedge for a while, she'll have lost all her body heat. Ah, look... I think she's rousing."

The kitten was still flopped on the towel but she'd raised her head and had turned towards the sound of Edie's mum's voice. She definitely looked more awake. And this time, when she tried to mew, she managed to make a noise. A definite, hungry little meow.

"OK!" Edie's mum laughed. "Let's see if we can get some milk into her." She picked up the box of milk powder and a little feeding bottle that she'd found in the cupboard. "This is kitten milk – it's meant to be like her mum's milk, it has all the right nutrients. If she's five weeks old, she should still be feeding from her mum. She'll be starting to eat solid food as well, but we'll stick with milk for now."

She spooned milk powder into the bottle and added warm water, stirring it around.

"That isn't very much," Edie pointed out.

"I know – but she may not want to take it. And we can always make more. Later on we'll weigh her, so we know exactly how much milk she should have but let's see what she thinks of the bottle first. Some kittens don't really like bottles, it probably feels a bit weird."

Edie watched anxiously as her mum lifted the kitten out of the box.

"You sit down," her mum suggested. "We'll put her on your knee and I'll hold the bottle." She laid the kitten on Edie's lap, stretched out on her front so she looked like a furry ginger frog. Then she tickled the kitten under her little white chin and laughed when the kitten stretched her head up. "That's it, sweetie pie. Here. What's this?" Very gently, Mum squeezed the bottle so a little milk dribbled out on to the kitten's neon-pink nose and dripped into her mouth.

The kitten blinked and then a darker pink tongue lapped out and licked the milk. She lifted up a paw eagerly, as if she was trying to grab the bottle, and Edie giggled in relief. She definitely liked the milk! Surely that was a good sign?

"Here you go," Edie's mum murmured, pushing the bottle's teat carefully into the kitten's tiny mouth. "Try that."

The kitten wasn't very good at it. She kept pawing at the bottle and accidentally pulling the teat out of her mouth, and she looked very grumpy about the whole thing, as though the milk just wasn't happening fast enough.

"Is she trying to hold on to the bottle?" Edie asked. She was still giggling. Even though she knew that she should be worried about the kitten's cut neck and paw, and Mum had said that the kitten was too tiny to be away from her mother, she couldn't help it. The kitten was just so funny.

"No, I think she's doing that because it's what she'd do to her mother if she was feeding from her. Kittens knead at their mum's teats to make the milk come faster."

"So she's trying to get it to come out of the bottle quicker! Greedy," Edie told the kitten, running one finger lightly down the fur on her back. It was the first time she'd stroked her, she realized. She loved stroking cats, but she'd been so busy rescuing this one, she hadn't given her even a little stroke till now.

"Once we've fed her, we need to clean up her wounds," Edie's mum said, gently moving the fur around the kitten's cut neck. "Actually, you know what, Edie, you hold the bottle.

I'll clean them up while she's busy with the milk and then hopefully she won't be upset about what I'm doing."

Edie watched worriedly as her mum got cotton wool and warm water, and started to clean the cut on her neck. Surely it would hurt? But the kitten only twitched a little and went back to chewing on the bottle of milk.

"Does it need stitches?" Edie asked.

"No, we'll be OK with glue… I think there's some of that in the kitchen cupboard, too…" Edie's mum grinned at her. "I know, I know. There's enough for a surgery in those cupboards. But it's useful stuff to have around. Just lift her up a minute, I want to pour on some antiseptic and you don't want it all down you, too."

She whisked another towel under the kitten and then poured antiseptic wash all over her neck.

"Aww, her fur's gone all spiky!"

"Yes, and you can see how little she really is," her mum said grimly. "Without all that fluffy fur."

"But she is drinking the milk, Mum. That's a good sign, isn't it?"

"Mmm."

"What are you two doing?"

Edie jumped as her dad appeared in the kitchen doorway.

"Must be something exciting, you didn't even hear me come in!" He leaned over to look. "Oh, where did this come from?" He looked around as if he expected to find a few more kittens scattered around the kitchen.

"I found her, Dad! Me and Layla
rescued her! She was stuck on some
barbed wire. She's really little. Mum
thinks she's only about five weeks old."
Edie looked up at him excitedly and
then frowned. Her mum and dad were
giving each other a Look. Not a good
look. "What?" she asked worriedly.

"She's very tiny, Edie love."

"I know. Mum said. But at least she's eating."

"Yeah…" Her dad sighed. "OK. Yes, that's good. But … kittens do just fade sometimes, if they've had a bad start. Don't look at me like that, Edie, I'm not trying to be mean. I just don't want you falling in love with a gorgeous kitten and then being heartbroken."

"Well, what else am I supposed to do?" Edie said, a bit crossly. It was all very well Mum and Dad both going on and on about how little and fragile the kitten was. Did they think she should have just left her stuck on that wire? "And I had to bring her home! Now isn't this the best possible house for a

39

sick kitten to be in? She's got *two* vets to help her!"

"OK, OK." Edie's mum hugged her carefully so as not to disturb the kitten. "Of course we're not saying you shouldn't have rescued her. We just don't want you to be upset…"

"If something happens to her…" Edie's voice wobbled a bit. "*If* something happens … of course I'll be upset. But at least I'll know I tried!"

# Chapter Four

Edie helped her mum weigh the kitten and work out exactly how much milk she ought to be having. Luckily the kitten was sleepy after the bottle she'd had so it wasn't that hard to get her to sit in the kitchen scales. She was so little, she fitted perfectly into the bowl.

"In a couple of days, if she's doing OK, we can introduce her to a bit of solid food," Edie's mum explained. "But for now, we're going to need to feed her milk six times a day."

"Six!" Edie squeaked.

"Yup. Every four hours. So, let's say … at six, ten and two in the day and six, ten and two at night."

"Two o'clock in the morning." Edie's dad sighed. "It'll be like having you all over again, Edie."

Because she'd already had a feed at five, Edie's mum and dad reckoned that the kitten wouldn't need another lot of milk at six. They'd feed her just before they went to bed and then get up again to feed her at two.

Edie called Layla to tell her how well the kitten was doing and that she was going to be given milk every four hours, including during the night. Layla agreed that she wouldn't mind getting up at two in the morning either. She loved cats and she'd wanted one for ages, but her dad wasn't all that keen on having a pet.

Edie peered into the kitten box as she got up to go to bed. She hadn't wanted to leave the kitten on her own in the kitchen, so the box was on the sofa between her and her mum. They'd been watching TV together, with the kitten snoozing in the middle.

"I'll set my alarm," she said.

"You don't need to get up at two in the morning!" Edie's mum hugged her. "I'll feed her, or your dad will. We can take turns doing the night feeds."

Edie shook her head.

"No, Mum! I rescued her." She frowned, trying to think how to put it.

"I can't leave you to look after her – it's important. I want to do it."

Her mum sighed. "OK. You can help at two, if you go to bed and go to sleep *now*."

Edie put her arms round her mum. "Thank you!"

Her dad laughed. "I bet you won't feel like that at two in the morning."

Actually, Edie felt surprisingly wide-awake. The beeping of her alarm clock

**44**

broke into a dream about the kitten, where she wouldn't stop mewing and Edie knew exactly why she had to get up. The kitten would be getting hungry. Perhaps she actually was mewing for real?

Edie pulled a jumper on over her pyjamas and hurried down the stairs. She could see a faint light from the kitchen – Mum or Dad must be down there already.

Her dad turned to her, smiling, as she came into the kitchen. "Wow, I wasn't sure you'd make it."

Edie made a face at him. Her dad was always teasing her about how long it took her to get up in the morning. "How is she? Did she mind being left alone?" Edie peered into the box and saw the kitten was staring back at her, green eyes round and worried. She looked a little bit less fragile than she had that afternoon – less floppy and exhausted – but the bandage around her paw made Edie's stomach twist. It was so sad to see the tiny kitten hurt and still frightened.

Edie's dad handed her the bottle. "She's fine – she was still fast asleep when I came down. Do you want to feed her? Do you think you can sit her on your knee and hold the bottle, too?"

"Definitely." Edie nodded and sat down, and her dad lifted the kitten out of the box for her. The little creature half-sprawled on Edie's lap but she wasn't relaxed – Edie could feel how tense she was, as though she was ready to spring away and escape. She was so tiny she wouldn't get anywhere, but she was still thinking about it. It was so sad.

"Don't worry," Edie whispered. "We just want to look after you."

Very gently, Edie held the bottle to the kitten's mouth and the kitten wriggled a little to reach it. She was so light, Edie could hardly feel the weight of her moving. But when the kitten started to suck, she was so determined, so focused on drinking that milk – even if she did still keep gnawing at the bottle and missing it and stomping her little paws on Edie's leg. The milk was hers and no one was taking it away.

Edie watched her sucking, feeling the rhythm as the kitten pulled on

the bottle. It was soothing. Sleepy.
She swallowed a yawn and realized
that her dad was helping her hold
the bottle. "I'm OK," she
muttered, sitting up a
bit straighter.

"I know you
are. It's still
the middle
of the night,
though.
You're allowed to
be a bit sleepy."

"I'm not going back to
bed!" Edie told him, and then she
looked guilty as the kitten stopped
feeding and tensed up. "Sorry, baby.
Shh."

"Let's go and sit on the sofa," Dad

suggested. "Come on." He scooped the kitten gently off Edie's lap and Edie followed him into the living room. The kitten reached eagerly for the bottle as soon as Edie held it for her, and Edie leaned against her dad's shoulder, watching the tiny pink muzzle and the kitten's contented, half-closed eyes. She ran one finger over the kitten's head and round her ears, stroking the silky ginger fur.

"Dad, listen…" Edie put her hand on his arm. "Listen, she's purring."

The kitten had almost stopped sucking now. She was sleepy, just licking at the bottle as if she was full and couldn't really be bothered. And there was a definite soft, tiny noise. A little purr.

The kitten felt the bottle move away from her mouth and she stirred, reaching after it, but then she slumped back down on to the soft fabric. She didn't want the milk that much. She was warm, snuggled on the girl's lap, and her stomach was nicely full.

Sleepily, as if the thought was far away, she wondered where her mother was and why she hadn't come back to find her. But she'd been fed, the way her mother fed her, and she was warm and clean and cared for.

The girl rubbed gently at her ears and the kitten began to purr.

"She looks so different." Layla leaned over the box and giggled as the kitten looked up at her. "I mean, she's properly awake. And the cut on her neck looks much better now." Layla eyed the kitten thoughtfully, and she gave a huge yawn, showing tiny white teeth. "Is it stupid to say that she looks fatter? I think she does, though it's only been a couple of days since we found her. But I think she looks fatter than when I came over yesterday…"

"Mum reckons she might not have been getting a lot to eat. If her mum was a feral cat, and she had lots of kittens, it would have been hard for her to make enough milk. But now she's getting this special kitten milk and it's got all these added vitamins.

It's like perfect kitten food." Edie gave the kitten a proud look. "She *does* seem fatter."

"Does your mum…" Layla wrinkled her nose, as if she wasn't quite sure how to say it. "Is she…"

"Is she still saying the kitten might not make it?" Edie sighed. "Yes. But not as much as before. And even Mum's impressed by the amount she's eating."

"We have to give her a name!" Edie said suddenly. "I can't keep just calling her 'she'. I didn't want to before, with everything Mum and Dad were saying, because it would be worse if we'd given her a name. Just look at her, though… She's so beautiful and she needs a name."

"She does," Layla agreed. "But are you sure she's a girl kitten? I thought ginger cats were usually boys."

"That's true," Edie said. "I just always thought she looked like a girl kitten. Maybe because of the long fur? And I was right! Mum told me she's definitely a girl."

They gazed at the kitten admiringly.

She *was* beautiful. When they'd first found her, she'd been so bedraggled and miserable-looking that Edie had hardly noticed her markings. And she'd only seen the kitten's long fur as something that had got her caught up on the barbed wire. But now, clean and well fed, the kitten's coat was fluffy and rich, and her nose was a beautiful bright pink, the same colour as her paw pads. She had long, long white whiskers and a whitish chin, but that was the only white on her. Even her tummy was a pale creamy oat colour.

"You could call her Fluff. She's the fluffiest thing I've ever seen!" Layla said, carefully reaching in a hand and tapping her fingers on the towel for the kitten to track. She wasn't quite at the pouncing stage yet but she was definitely watching.

"Mmm. Maybe." Edie frowned. "I'd like something that was a bit more special, sort of different. Like Treasure, or … or Rescue. Because we found her."

Layla nodded. "I know what you mean. Oh! I know." She laughed. "You could call her Barbie. Because of the barbed wire!"

Edie looked at the kitten again. "Yes! That's perfect! She does look like a Barbie. Yes, Barbie, that's you," she murmured lovingly to the kitten. Then she sighed. "I wish we knew where she came from."

Layla glanced at the living-room

door – they could hear Edie's mum and dad chatting in the kitchen.

"Are you going to keep her?" she whispered. "I mean, we've just given her a name. What if she has to go and live with someone else?"

Edie smiled. "I think it's going to be OK. Mum came downstairs on Saturday morning, and me and Dad and the kitten – I mean, Barbie – we were all asleep on the sofa. We'd fallen asleep feeding her! And she was asleep on both of us, half on me and half on Dad. Mum laughed and said something like, *Well, she's obviously not going anywhere, is she?* And I reckon that means we're keeping her."

She reached out and gave Layla a quick hug. "But you can come and see

her whenever,
I promise. You
rescued her,
too."

Layla sniffed
and sighed.
"Thanks. Hey,
we'd better get to
school." She leaned
over to rub Barbie
under her chin. "Bye, gorgeous."

# Chapter Five

"This is almost where we found her,"
Edie murmured, stopping to look
around the path, trying to work out
exactly where it had been. "Yes – here,
look." They could see where the grass
had been squashed down as they
crouched to rescue the little kitten.

Edie took a shocked breath at the
sight of the rusty, jagged wire. It was

hard to think of Barbie being caught up on it, even when she knew that the kitten was safe now. She had just left her at home, with Dad teaching her how to pat her little paws at a piece of string. She was the world's best looked-after kitten, Edie was making sure of it.

"We should go, we'll be late," Layla pointed out.

Edie took one last look around. "I hate thinking of her stuck here," she said, with a shiver. "Do you think we could stop on the way home? Look for clues? We should try and find out where she came from."

Layla nodded. "Course. Though I don't know what we're looking for."

Edie sighed. "Me neither. I just feel like we ought to."

Edie had printed out a photo that her mum had taken of her feeding Barbie, and she spent the whole of break and lunch showing it off to everyone in their class. It was great having everyone *oohing* and *aahing* over how cute and fluffy and little she was but Edie felt worried all day. She hadn't liked leaving Barbie with Dad – even though he was a vet and she knew he could look after a kitten much better than she could. He was even going to take Barbie into work with him later on so she wouldn't be left on her own. All the same, Edie still felt like she was abandoning her tiny cat. She was practically chasing Layla out of the cloakroom after school.

"Slow down!" Layla gasped, as she hurried along the path after Edie.

"I can't! I really, really want to get home and check Barbie's OK, *and* I want to look at the place we found her and see if we can work out what happened," Edie explained.

Layla smiled. "Oh, all right." She sped up a bit, until they arrived panting back at the little space in the bushes. "I honestly don't see what we're going to find, though."

Edie sighed. "I know. But we have to try. I mean, what if it was the cat's owner who abandoned her kittens?"

"How horrible!" Layla was shocked.

"Some people do that. They don't think animals matter." Edie scowled and Layla stared at her.

"You look scary like that."

"Good!" But then Edie's shoulders drooped. "I can't see any clues, can you? And we don't even know what we're looking for."

Layla stood on tiptoe, trying to peer through the bushes on the side of the footpath. "What's behind this hedge?"

"The road that goes into the village." Edie stepped up close to the hedge. "If Mum's right and it was a feral cat moving her kittens, she would have had to carry them across the road."

"Maybe a car…" Layla's voice trailed off, and the two girls looked at each other, appalled. "But your mum or dad would know about that, wouldn't they? Somebody would have brought the cat in if they'd hit her?"

"I suppose…" Edie sniffed. "Can you see anything else? On the other side it's just a field…"

"There are some sheds or something over there, near that copse of trees." Layla pointed across the field. "They're quite a long way, though." Then she glanced up at the sky. "Edie, look! It's going to pour down any minute. Come on. Let's get home."

Edie watched the grey-black cloud chasing up behind them and nodded. It looked like it might thunder and she knew Layla hated thunderstorms. Besides, she was desperate to get home and see Barbie. She grabbed Layla's hand and they ran down the length of the field and across the courtyard.

Edie's dad was standing at their front door and he waved. "I'm glad you're back – it looks like it's going to pour down, the kitchen went so dark!"

"How's Barbie?" Edie asked, panting a little.

"Hello, Dad, did you have a nice day, Dad…" Edie's dad rolled his eyes. "Barbie's fine. She's started to eat the kitten food. And she got a lot of fussing from Sammi and Jo at the surgery."

Edie smiled. The two receptionists were both big cat fans, she wasn't surprised they'd loved Barbie.

Barbie was in her box on the kitchen table, where Dad had been starting to make the dinner. She was awake and standing up, although she looked a bit wobbly.

"Hello, beautiful," Edie whispered, putting her hand into the box. She didn't want to scare the tiny cat by suddenly stroking her.

Barbie looked up at the hand that had appeared in her box and stomped forwards, marching shakily across the folded towel, her tiny paws catching on the fabric. When she got to Edie's hand, she butted at it hard with the side of her head and mewed.

Layla started laughing and pulled her phone out of her backpack. "I promised I'd take a video of her," she explained. "My little sister loves cats. And my mum said Barbie sounded cute." She rolled her eyes. "I'm still working on my dad. But I don't think even he could resist *you*," she added to Barbie.

Barbie rubbed her tiny face against Edie's hands and purred. It seemed far too loud a noise for such a tiny kitten to make.

Edie's dad sighed. "Typical. I've been looking after her all day, and she didn't do any of that to me! She's obviously decided you're her person."

Edie looked at him sideways. "Dad … now she's better, can we keep her? You and Mum didn't really say for definite the other day…"

"She's keeping *us*. Look at her. Yes, Edie, don't worry, she's staying."

Barbie nudged lovingly at the girl, rubbing up against her hand and

scenting her properly. Now everyone
would know that Edie was hers.

Then she gave a surprised little
squeak as she was gently lifted out
of the box and Edie snuggled her up
against the cardigan she was wearing.
Barbie sniffed at it curiously and stuck
her tiny claws into the fabric, pulling
herself up like a mountain climber.

It was hard work
but she climbed
all the way
to Edie's
shoulder and
batted a paw
at Edie's
plait, which
was swinging
temptingly

next to her. It was so close – she could reach it if she stretched out, just a little. Barbie leaned over a bit further and her paws slid on the cardigan. She could feel herself slipping down and she scrabbled frantically for a second, and mewed.

Edie's hand closed round her tummy, scooping her up again and setting her gently back in her safe box. The kitten yawned and slumped down, her front paws splayed out against the soft towel. She wriggled a little and breathed out a tiny, squeaky snore.

# Chapter Six

"Look, there's a rainbow!" Layla pointed out of the kitchen window. "It's really sunny and beautiful outside now."

Edie came to stand beside her. "Amazing! Hey, do you want to come out searching for Barbie's family again? I can't help worrying about them – I mean, if there are other kittens and the mum had to abandon them, too… They could be out there on their own."

"Because she couldn't feed them? Would she do that?" asked Layla.

Edie sighed. "I don't know. We still don't know what happened to Barbie. I just hate thinking of kittens being hungry and cold."

"Yeah…" Layla nodded. "Let's try again."

"Maybe we should look in other places – all round the field and in that little copse nearby."

"That's a long way from where we found Barbie," Layla said doubtfully.

"I know but you just saw her climb up my cardigan and she's only five weeks old! Mother cats do amazing stuff to look after their kittens. She might have carried them for miles. She'd have had to keep putting them down and leaving them – she can only carry one in her mouth at a time – so it would have taken ages but they can do it."

"Mmm. Maybe…" Layla nodded. "OK. Should we tell your dad?"

Edie nodded and went to find him in the little office space under the stairs. "Dad, me and Layla are going to look for Barbie's mum."

He looked round. "OK… But if you find her, don't touch her, will you? Feral cats can be fierce, especially if they're protecting their kittens. Where are you going to look?"

"Round the edges of the field and in the copse?"

Edie's dad checked his watch. "OK, but I want you back by five thirty – so you've got just over an hour. And don't go on the road."

"We won't!" Edie hurried out before her dad could change his mind. She was allowed to go off exploring with Layla and her other friends, but she had a feeling Dad didn't really like it. He worried too much.

"We could start by checking the hedges all round this field," she suggested to Layla. They were standing in a corner of it. "She might just have made a nest in the bushes."

It sounded simple enough, but the field was enormous and the rain had left the grass soaking wet. By the time they were halfway round, the girls were drenched and feeling a bit hopeless. They hadn't seen any sign of a mother cat or more kittens.

"What about those sheds?" Edie asked suddenly. The buildings were over on the far side of the next field near a copse of trees and looked like they'd been abandoned for a while – she could see holes in all the roofs.

"Do you think it's OK?" Layla said doubtfully. "Mum always says not to go inside anywhere like that, in case it's dangerous."

"I know, my mum and dad say the same. We won't go inside – we'll just look around."

"All right," Layla agreed.

They worked their way round the corner of the big field to a gap in the hedge and then round the next field to the tumbledown buildings. They walked into a yard with old sheds on three sides.

"I think this used to be part of the same farm that our houses were in," Edie said. "Mum said it was a machine store or something. But it's really falling down."

Layla peered carefully at the walls and the open doorways. "We could just put our heads round the doors," she suggested. "That would be OK."

The old sheds seemed to have been abandoned for a long time. They were almost completely empty, with just a few bits of dusty equipment here and there. But in the smallest and least falling down of the three buildings, there was a pile of old sacks, and on them was a gingery, furry bundle of kittens.

Edie and Layla forgot completely about being safe and never going inside abandoned buildings. They crept as quietly as they could into the shed, and crouched down by the squirming mass of fur.

"How many?" Edie whispered.

"Um, three, I think? No … four? It's really hard to tell when they're all on top of each other. No, it *is* three, look, that leg belongs to that one." Layla pressed her hand over her mouth, trying not to laugh out loud and disturb the kittens. "They're so sweet – oh, they're waking up! Sorry, kittens…"

The kittens were wriggling even more now, starting to climb on top of each other, so it was even harder to see which paws and tails went where. One of them was ginger like Barbie, but with shorter fur, and the other two were mostly black, but flecked and spotted with ginger.

"These have to be Barbie's brothers or sisters," Edie said. "Actually, two sisters and one brother, I think."

Layla frowned. "You're making that up!"

"I'm not! You know everyone thinks ginger kittens are boys? And actually, you can have ginger girl cats like Barbie, it's just rarer? Well, I asked Mum to explain it to me again, and she said it's super-rare to have a tortoiseshell boy cat. And two of these are tortoiseshell." She pointed to the two kittens currently squirming on top of the ginger one. "And the ginger one is *probably* a boy."

"Oh… OK. Well, whatever they are they're gorgeous. And the tortoiseshell ones are so pretty. Look! This one's got a ginger streak down her nose!"

"They don't look like they've been

abandoned, do they?" Edie looked around the shed. "This is a nest that their mum's put them in, and they're really plump and lively. She must be off hunting for food." She turned to look out of the door. "I think Mum was right about what happened. Barbie can't have wandered off from here and ended up caught on that fence, not by herself. Her mum must have had to move the kittens, but Barbie got stuck." Edie's voice shook a little. "Her mum had to choose between her and the others. She had to get her kittens somewhere safe."

"She wouldn't have been able to get Barbie off that wire either." Layla sighed. "Wow. I wonder where she had to carry them from? And trying to do the journey four times with four kittens!"

"Every time she put one down to go and get the others, they must have been trying to wriggle away all over the place. She would have hated it. Poor cat, it must have been so horrible for her. Imagine having to leave your baby behind…"

# Chapter Seven

"Layla, look…" Evie whispered, gently turning her friend round. "In the doorway."

Watching them, frozen at the entrance of the shed, was a tiny black cat. She didn't look big enough or old enough to have had kittens, Edie thought. She was so skinny and little, but she had the most beautiful golden-green eyes.

"Shuffle back!" Edie told Layla. "I think she's scared to come in because we're here." Her mum had told her how shy feral cats could be. The kittens were too little to be scared but their mum wouldn't want to come near people.

Slowly, carefully, the two girls wriggled back to the side wall of the shed, as far away from the kittens and the mother cat as they could get. Edie wished they could just leave, but the kittens' mum was in the doorway. She had her ears laid back flat, and she was pressed against the side of the door as if she was terrified – but she didn't run away. She was obviously desperate to get to her kittens.

"She's shaking," Layla whispered.

"I know… Maybe if we keep still
she'll come in and then we can get out
of the door without scaring them."

The cat watched them suspiciously,
glancing back and forth between them
and her kittens as if she still wasn't
sure it was safe to move. Then, at last,
she darted across the shed to her nest
on the old sacks. She huddled herself
over her kittens, as if she thought
she needed to protect them from the

two girls. Then she leaned down and picked up the ginger kitten in her mouth, hauling him out of the nest by the scruff of his neck.

Layla gasped. "She's hurting him!"

"No," Edie whispered. "That's just how they carry their kittens. Look, he's gone all limp. I don't think it hurts. But where's she moving him to?" She looked worriedly at Layla. "I think she's doing this because of us! We scared her, and now she thinks this place isn't safe and she has to take them somewhere new."

The cat didn't seem to know what to do. She jumped up on to an old wooden crate that was behind the nest, with the kitten dangling from her mouth, but then she hesitated and jumped down again, putting the kitten back with his sisters. She padded around the little pile of sacks, looking over at the girls every so often and then nudging worriedly at her kittens.

"Let's get out of here," Edie suggested, breathing into Layla's ear. "We'll stay by the wall and try to be really quick. Yes?"

Layla nodded, and they scurried as quickly as they could round the side of the shed and out of the door. Edie looked back as they dashed out and saw the mother cat still staring after them anxiously.

"What if she moves them and they get hurt like Barbie did?" Edie said, as they stood in the long grass outside the shed. "Where's she even going to take them? She had to go so far last time, all the way across two fields and the road at least. It's so dangerous!"

"We were trying to help…" Layla said, her voice faltering.

"And I think we've just made everything worse." Edie shook her head. "We shouldn't have stayed looking at the kittens. But they were so cute, I didn't think about the mother cat coming back and getting scared. We should have gone away and got some food for her and left them alone." She bit her bottom lip. "We messed up. Can I borrow your phone to ring my dad? Maybe he'll know what to do."

Layla nodded, pulling the phone out of her pocket and handing it to Edie.

It had been her birthday present and Edie was definitely planning to ask for a phone for her birthday, too. "Dad?" she gasped, as soon as he picked up. "Dad, we've found Barbie's mum and the other kittens. They're in the old machine sheds, across the field from where we found Barbie. But I think we scared her, she's going to move the kittens, and we don't know what to do…"

"Wow!" her dad murmured. "OK." He paused and Edie could almost hear him thinking. "Right. I reckon we need to get them all to a shelter.

They probably won't be able to rehome the mum, not if she's feral, but they could find homes for the kittens once they're not feeding from her any more. They're still young enough to get used to people. So … we need to catch the mum and the kittens before she moves them again."

"She's really nervous, Dad. I don't think she's going to be easy to catch."

"I know, but we'll bribe her. I'll bring a cat cage and some good snacks. Your mum's going to wonder what's happened to the contents of the fridge. We just need to find out what she likes. I'm betting on cheese. Lots of cats can't resist cheese. But you never know, it could be cold baked beans! I'll bring those, too, just in case."

Edie laughed shakily. She could tell that her dad was being funny on purpose, to try and calm her down.

"Don't worry, Edie. We'll manage. And it's wonderful that you and Layla found them. I honestly didn't think that you would. See you in ten."

"Bye. Thanks, Dad." Edie handed the phone back to Layla with a sigh of relief. "He's going to come and catch them, and take them to a shelter." Then she glanced around, pulling a face. "And then he'll know we went inside this falling-down old shed. Maybe he won't mind because we were so clever and found the kittens."

Layla rolled her eyes. "I know… I've probably lost all my pocket money for about a month. But it was worth it."

Barbie stood up with her paws on the side of her box, mewing hopefully at Edie's dad. It was only a little while since she'd been fed, but she was wide awake and wanted to get out of the box. She could hear him moving around, opening and shutting the door that led into the garage, and then the squeak of the door to the fridge.

She mewed again, a sharp, demanding squeak. If Edie had been there, she would have come running to see what was the matter. She would have picked her up, and petted her and let her play on the kitchen floor, patting bottle tops around and climbing all over her lap. Edie's dad was ignoring her.

Barbie scrabbled at the side of
the box and sank her claws into the
thick cardboard.

It was a new
box, bigger
than her first
one, and it
had taller
sides. But
if she tried
hard enough...
Determinedly, she
hopped and hauled
herself up to the edge and mewed,
half-scared, half-triumphant as she
wobbled on the side of the box.

Edie's dad looked round and saw
her, just as she scrambled and jumped
to the kitchen floor. "Perfect," he

murmured, scooping her up and popping her back in. "Just when I have to go and rescue the rest of your family, you decide it's time to learn how to escape from your box. Brilliant timing, kitten. Sorry, but I'm not taking you with me. No, don't just climb out again!"

But Barbie was already climbing up the side of the box and Edie's dad looked around the kitchen, trying to work out if there was anything she could hurt herself on if he left her. There weren't any gaps she could get stuck in and there was no way she could get out of the doors. With a sigh, he grabbed a piece of paper and some Sellotape and scribbled a quick note to warn Edie's mum:

*Free range kitten!*

Then he closed the kitchen door behind him and taped it up where she'd see it before she opened the door.

"Dad!" Edie waved as she saw the car bumping down the lane that led the long way round back to their house. She pointed to the overgrown yard in front of the sheds, but her dad stopped the car in the lane instead.

"I'll leave it here, I don't reckon anyone's going to be coming past and I don't want to scare the cat any more. Where is she?" he added, as he got a wire crate out of the back of the car and a bag of food to bait it with.

"They're all inside this shed." Edie pulled him into the yard and across to the doorway.

"This isn't the kind of place you two should be exploring," Edie's dad pointed out, glancing around and then eyeing the two girls.

"I know – and we never would usually…" Edie said apologetically and Layla nodded.

"We only meant to look round the door…" she said.

"And then we saw the kittens," added Edie. "They're gorgeous, Dad, look."

Edie's dad peered cautiously through the doorway and smiled. "Three of them, right? They're all walking around now. I can't see the mum, though."

"I know, after we called you, we went on watching them from the door – the mum kept picking the kittens up in her mouth and putting them down again, and then she disappeared into this pile of old boxes and stuff at the back of the shed. That was a few minutes ago. Now the kittens are starting to wake up and mew, and one of them's wandering round the shed crying for her but she hasn't come back."

"There are lots of holes in the walls," Layla put in. "She could have gone without us seeing her. Maybe we just scared her off and she's left."

Edie swallowed hard. "What if we made her leave all her kittens behind?"

# Chapter Eight

Behind a pile of old wooden crates, the black cat sat shivering. She didn't know what to do. She was desperately hungry and she could smell food, just there, so close… But her kittens! The talking and scuffling and banging must mean danger for them, and she couldn't get close enough to pick up even one of them and run. She would wait. She had to, even though it made her whiskers itch with fear.

And all the time there was that delicious smell of food. If only she could eat, she would be able to feed the kittens better. She could even bite off some little bits of food for them, too. It was time they were learning… Perhaps she could just get close enough to snatch the food and run? But she could still hear the voices, rising higher. Her ears flattened back and she squirmed away, closer to the wall.

"I don't think the mother cat would leave her kittens," Edie's dad said gently, putting his arm round Edie's shoulders to hug her. "She's probably just a bit spooked by you two turning up. Don't panic."

"Should we put the kittens in the cage?" Edie asked. "Maybe that would tempt her to come and look, too… Or it might just scare her off." She sighed.

"It's tricky to know," her dad agreed. "Show me where you think she went."

Edie and Layla crept back into the shed, and Edie's dad laughed at the three kittens. The ginger boy was sitting on the sacks, making loud squeaky mews, obviously wanting his mother to come back and feed him. But the two tortoiseshell girls were stomping about the shed, batting at bits of straw. Then they both decided that they wanted the same tiny piece of stick, and pounced on it. One of the kittens whipped it from her sister, who jumped on top of her, trying to wrestle it away.

"Typical." Edie's dad shook his head. "Naughty torties."

"What?" Edie stared at him.

Her dad laughed. "I don't know if it's really true but tortoiseshell cats have a reputation of being … um … determined? Stubborn? What your grandma would call a bit of a character. So, naughty tortie."

"I think they're gorgeous," Layla said indignantly. "They're only babies."

"Shh, look!" Edie grabbed her dad's arm. "I just saw her, the mum! She's behind those wooden crates."

"OK. Let's try putting the cage over there then, with a trail of food to tempt her…" Edie's dad suggested. He opened the bag he'd brought and pulled out a packet of cocktail sausages that were meant for Edie's packed lunches. "I knew you wouldn't mind," he said, showing her the pack. "If she doesn't go for these we'll try cheese."

"She looks hungry enough to eat anything," Edie whispered. "Oh, I hope this works." She watched eagerly as her dad laid a couple of sausages close to the boxes where the cat was hiding and then a few more inside the cage.

"I need to stay fairly close because I've got to shut the door once she goes in," her dad explained. "If this is no good I'll get the local cat shelter out, they'll have a trap cage we can use. But I shouldn't think they'll be able to come today."

"She might have moved the kittens by the time they get here," Edie pointed out, and her dad nodded.

"Yes, so let's hope we can tempt her in now."

But the black cat stayed stubbornly away from the sausages. Edie was sure that she could see her pacing back and forth in the shadows behind all the junk but she wouldn't come out. She didn't appear when her dad added cheese to the trail of bait either.

"This is not looking good," he said, after about half an hour of waiting. The kittens were all mewing miserably now and they sounded really hungry. He looked around, frowning. "I wonder if it's worth putting the cage round the back of the shed instead? There's a pretty big hole in the wall there. We could put the cage up against it. Maybe she'd go for the food if she couldn't see us?"

He picked up the cage and the girls followed him round to the back of the shed. The wooden wall had several rotten pieces crumbling away and there was a hole that looked a perfect cat-door size. Edie's dad put the cage close to the hole, and stood flat against the wall, ready to swing the door shut.

"Dad, I've just thought of something!" Edie whispered urgently. "Layla's got a video of Barbie on her phone and Barbie's mewing really loudly in it. If we played it, do you think the mum might come? Would she know it was Barbie? She'd come and see, wouldn't she?"

"She might…" her dad said slowly. "It's worth a try, anyway."

Layla pulled out her phone and crouched against the wall on the other side of the cage. She started the video, turned the sound right up and held the phone just by the side of the hole. Barbie's squeaky mew echoed around them and Edie looked hopefully at the hole. Surely her mother wouldn't be able to resist?

After a moment, there was a rustling on the other side of the wall. Edie made frantic faces at her dad, pointing to the hole, and he nodded back. Layla set the video to play again, and black whiskers appeared at the hole, followed by a black nose and then the rest of the cat, her ears twitching cautiously. She looked around for her kitten, and then sniffed the sausages and cheese, the first piece just inside the open cage.

Edie and Layla stood frozen against the wall of the shed as the cat stepped forward. She obviously couldn't resist the food right in front of her and she gobbled down the first sausage in seconds. Then she walked right into the cage to eat the rest of them – and Edie's dad swung the cage door shut.

"Look at you, you're so clever," Edie murmured, as Barbie sat up on her bottom and waved her front paws at the feathery toy. Edie had spotted it in the supermarket while she was out shopping with her mum the day before, and it was Barbie's new favourite thing. It was like a mini feather duster, a bendy wand topped with lime green feathers and tinselly bits, and the little kitten loved the way it bounced. She danced about all over the kitchen chasing it.

"And you're getting so big… I don't know how you can be so different in just a week. I wonder how your brother and sisters are doing?" Edie said, flicking up the feathers and giggling as Barbie sprang into the air. She was learning to do the most amazing standing leaps – she could jump twice her own height when she really tried. "Do you think your sisters are being naughty torties, like Dad said? Layla thought they were gorgeous, but they're nowhere near as cute as you. Dad said the lady at the shelter thought they'd all be adopted easily, though. She said they'd do lots of work to socialize them, so they made good friendly pets."

The kittens' mum wouldn't ever be gentle enough to become a pet, though, which Edie thought was really sad. The shelter had said they would wait until the kittens were fully weaned and rehomed, which would be another couple of weeks, when they were about eight weeks old. Then they'd neuter their mum so she couldn't have any more kittens and release her back near where Edie and Layla had found her. Edie didn't like the idea of the black cat living outdoors again, in the cold and the rain, but Mum and Dad had said it was probably what she'd be happiest doing.

"Do you miss them?" Edie whispered, as Barbie gave a massive yawn, which showed a lot of her bright pink tongue. "Do you even remember them?"

Barbie sniffed at the green feathers,

which Edie was dancing in front of her nose again, and batted at them with one paw. She wasn't really trying. She'd been jumping and chasing for ages and now she was tired. She gave another huge yawn and padded over to Edie, climbing up her jeans and scrambling into her lap. She slumped down and then stood up again, marching round in a circle on Edie's tunic top until she had it just right. Then she curled herself into a little ginger ball, with one paw over her eyes and went to sleep.

"Guess what! Guess, you have to guess!" Layla was hopping up and down on the front doorstep, hardly able to get the words out, she was so excited.

"What? Oooh, catch her! Sneaky puss!" Edie and Layla both lunged for Barbie, who'd crept up behind Edie and was making a dash for the front door. Layla grabbed her and snuggled her up against her fleece.

"Well done," said Edie. "She's desperate to go outside but Mum and Dad say she can't until she's had all her vaccinations and she's been neutered. And that won't be for ages. She's got to be almost four months old before they do it."

Layla beamed back at her. "No problem. I need the practice," she said happily, glancing meaningfully between Edie and Barbie, who was now trying to climb up her fleece.

"Practice? Hey, come in before she disappears down the back of you and makes another run for it." Edie beckoned Layla inside and shut the door, and Barbie sprang down from Layla's arms and marched away in a kitten huff, tail whipping from side to side. Edie giggled. "I don't think she's talking to us now. Anyway, what are you so excited about?"

"I persuaded them! Actually, I think it was mostly Barbie. Remember when my mum and dad came over to have coffee with yours the other day and Barbie was playing, and then she spent all that time sitting on my dad's lap?"

"He did look pretty happy about it," Edie observed.

"He's never had a cat, he's always said he wasn't a cat person. But they know all about Barbie's sisters – I showed them the photos I took on my phone that day we found them, and so…"

"You're going to adopt one of the naughty torties?" Edie threw her arms round Layla. "That's amazing! Barbie's going to have her sister living next door!"

"We went to see them at the shelter yesterday afternoon and we're picking her up the weekend after next! They have to come and do a home visit first, and the kittens have to be eight weeks old to leave their mum."

"Which one? The one with more ginger, or the darker one?"

"This one." Layla showed Edie a photo on her phone – Layla holding a gorgeous tortoiseshell kitten against her shoulder. They were nose to nose and Edie thought she'd never seen her friend look so happy. "She's the dark one, but she's got a big ginger streak down her nose. And her whiskers are white on one side and black on the other!" She smiled blissfully. "Sorry, Edie, but I think she's even cuter than Barbie."

Edie grinned. "That's OK. But don't you listen to her, Barbie! She thinks your sister's more gorgeous than you are!" she added to her kitten, who'd forgotten to be cross and was marching back down the hall towards them, dragging a huge catnip-stuffed fish in her mouth. It was nearly as big as she was and she kept tripping over it. Eventually she just gave up and lay down on her side, hugging the fish and kicking at it with her hind paws.

Edie shook her head as she crouched down beside her. She tickled Barbie's cream-coloured tummy, and the ginger kitten gave up on the fish and came to nudge against Edie's arm, rubbing the side of her head up and down Edie's sleeve, and purring and purring.

"She really loves you," Layla murmured, and Edie smiled at her.

"Dad says it's because I'm the one who feeds her but he's only being grumpy."

"No, it's more than that. Do you think the tortoiseshell kitten will love me, too?" she added shyly. "I'm going to be looking after her." She reached out to run her hand over Barbie's ears and the kitten purred for her as well.

"Of course she will. It looks like she already does in that photo." Edie gathered Barbie up in her arms, gently combing her fingers through the kitten's long ginger fur. "Imagine if we hadn't stopped to find out what that noise was," she said, looking round at Layla wide-eyed. "We'd never have found them all."

"Best walk home from school ever," Layla said seriously and then she laughed as Barbie wriggled in Edie's arms so that she was snuggled in the crook of her elbow, on her back like a baby. Her pale ginger paws were folded on her chest, and she yawned, wide enough to show her needle-sharp white teeth. Then her green eyes closed slowly, and she breathed out a tiny, quiet purr.

Barbie batted a cautious paw at her new
cat flap. She had only been
allowed to go out for a
few days, and she was
still a bit confused by
the flap – the way it
sometimes opened
and sometimes
didn't – and she
didn't much like
the bang
it made
when it
shut behind her. She usually jumped
through it as fast as she could. She
patted it again and then dived through,
out into the garden.

It was sunny and warm, and there
were butterflies. She loved butterflies.

They were like the feathery toy that Edie waved for her – they bounced and fluttered, and she never knew which direction they would go in. She had tried chasing them, but they were hard to catch…

Barbie turned as she heard the back door open behind her, and Edie stepped out carrying a sandwich. Barbie eyed the plate hopefully. Edie was good at sharing, and her sandwiches often had ham in them, or cheese. She liked cheese. She padded over to Edie and started to weave around her feet.

"Layla!" Edie called across the garden. "Are you there? Is Amber out?" She hopped up on to the garden bench and looked over the wall.

"Yes! She's chasing butterflies, I really hope she doesn't catch one."

"Barbie loves doing that, too. Oh! Hello, Barbie!"

Barbie was scrabbling at the wall, and Edie watched impressed as she climbed all the way on to the top, next to Edie's elbow. The little kitten perched there looking proud of herself and Edie scratched her behind the ears.

"Aren't you clever? Look, who's that?" Edie whispered to her, pointing across Layla's garden. "Can you see?"

Barbie's tail fluffed up a bit and Edie watched her, a little worried. She wasn't sure how Barbie was going to feel about another cat so close to her own garden.

Amber came pacing down the garden towards the wall. There wasn't a bench on her side, so she couldn't jump up, but she stood beneath the wall, gazing up at Barbie, her golden eyes round and curious.

The two kittens stared at each other, and Edie and Layla stood watching. Neither of them had been sure how their kittens would react when they met. Would they even understand that they were sisters?

Then Amber stood up, patting her front paws against Layla's leg, asking to be picked up. Layla lifted her, and Amber leaned out of her arms, reaching forward curiously towards the wall.

Barbie leaned over, too, and the kittens sniffed at each other. Amber wriggled and Layla reached up to put her on the wall next to Barbie.

"Do you think they remember?" Edie whispered, as the sisters inspected each other carefully, sniffing and nudging. Then she smiled as Barbie stepped closer to Amber and rubbed her head all round Amber's, nuzzling at her gently. "They do, look! They know they're sisters!" Edie rested her chin on her arms, watching as Amber snuffled round Barbie, and smiled at Layla on the other side of the wall.

"We rescued them both," Layla whispered.

"We're never going to let anything happen to you," Edie told them. Then she laughed as Barbie padded back along the wall to nuzzle a cold little nose lovingly against her cheek.

A Kitten
Called Tiger

From best-selling author
HOLLY WEBB
Illustrated by Sophy Williams

# The Unwanted Puppy

From best-selling author

## HOLLY WEBB

Illustrated by Sophy Williams

## HOLLY WEBB

Holly Webb started out as a children's book editor and wrote her first series for the publisher she worked for. She has been writing ever since, with over one hundred books to her name. Holly lives in Berkshire, with her husband and three young sons. Holly's pet cats are always nosying around when she is trying to type on her laptop.

For more information about Holly Webb visit:

# www.holly-webb.com